0079

To Jennie
Merry Christmas
lots of love always

Dad.
xxxx.

STEVE AUGARDE

Barnaby Shrew, Black Dan and...

the Mighty Wedgwood

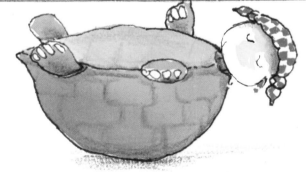

ANDRE DEUTSCH

First published 1979 by
André Deutsch Limited
105 Great Russell Street London WC1

Copyright © 1979 by Steve Augarde

Printed in Great Britain by
Sackville Press Billericay Ltd

British Library Cataloguing in Publication Data

Augarde, Steve
    Barnaby, Black Dan and the mighty Wedgwood.
    I. Title
    823'.9'1J   PZ10.3

    ISBN 0-233-97104-1

First published in the United States of America 1979

Library of Congress Number
79-53140

One of the good things about being a sailor (apart from sailing of course) is setting foot on dry land again when you've been away at sea for some time.

In the days of the old sailing ships, when you had to rely on the wind to puff you about from place to place, you couldn't be *that* sure that you ever *would* set foot on dry land again. So when you did it was cause for some celebration.

The good ship *Pied Piper* and her crew of sailor rats had been bobbing around the seven seas for a fairly long spell and now she was in dock again. It was time for a holiday.

Captain R. Jimlad Rat stood on the poop deck and addressed his crew.

"Rats!" he said, "I will be brief. Here we are, so off you go and ah . . . the LAST ONE DOWN THE PLANK'S A CISSY!" And away he sped, closely followed by his crew as you can see.

There's Captain Rat out in front, and that huge rat behind him is Great Big Harry (GBH for short), thought by many to be the biggest rat in the world. Then comes Mr Fred Friendly, the mate, followed by Barnaby Shrew the cabin shrew. (If you're wondering what Barnaby's carrying there, it's Wedgwood the tortoise. Wedgwood isn't a very good runner.) And finally, running in the wrong direction altogether, is Lookout Frank. He's the ship's lookout. He can't see very well but he's the only one who's not frightened to climb all the way up to the crow's nest. Probably because he can't see how far down it is.

Well there they go.

What a crew.

Ten minutes later they were all in the Merry Winkle – a tavern in the town. All, that is, except Lookout Frank. He was still trying to find the gangplank. Captain Rat and Mr Fred Friendly, the mate, were playing shove-doubloon, (a bit like shove-ha'penny but more expensive) with GBH chalking up the scores.

Barnaby Shrew and Wedgwood sat on two stools and played peanuts. This is very easy. You throw a peanut up into the air and try to catch it in your mouth. If you miss, you pick up the peanut and try again. You keep on doing this until you catch the peanut. Or until it gets so dusty you wouldn't want to eat it anyway.

A good time was being had by all, as they say, when the door burst open. Into the tavern strode another bunch of sailor rats.

Leading them was a big black rat dressed in brightly coloured clothes. He was wearing earrings and on his shoulder was a curious and fierce-looking parrot. The parrot was wearing an eye-patch and smoking a cigar.

There was no mistaking who this was. Barnaby had seen the black rat's picture stuck up on 'Definitely Not Wanted' posters everywhere.

It was Black Dan the Pirate and his fearsome parrot, Tough Eric!

Black Dan (so people said) ate a boiled leg for breakfast every day and he didn't much care whose it was!

Black Dan (so people said) once keel-hauled his own granny for forgetting to send him an easter egg!

Black Dan (so people said) had to nail his own boots to the floor to stop them trying to run away from him when he went to bed at night!

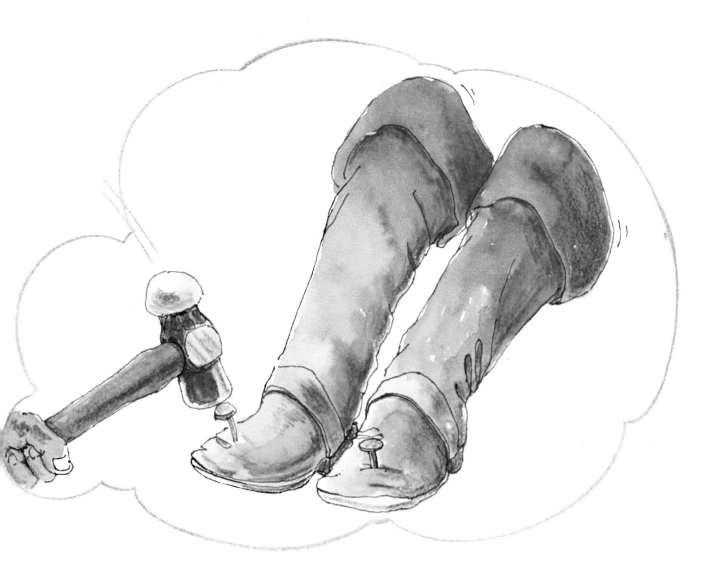

He was a terrible rat and his parrot (so people said) was just as bad and only encouraged him!

Well, Barnaby decided to get out of the way. He picked up Wedgwood the tortoise and started to clamber down from his stool.

Too late! Black Dan and his pirate crew were already at the bar.

"HAHARR!" cried Black Dan, spitting on the floor, "What have we got here then, eh?" He picked up Barnaby by his braces and plonked him back on his stool again. Then he struck a match on the back of Wedgwood's shell to light Tough Eric's cigar. He really did have the most dreadful manners.

"Hey!" shouted Captain Rat from the other side of the room, "That's our cabin shrew. You leave him alone!"

"HOHO!" said Black Dan, "It's a *shrew*, is it? I did wonder. And what's this thing here, his lunchbox?"

"That," said Captain Rat, walking over to the bar with GBH and Mr Fred Friendly, "is Wedgwood our ship's tortoise and er . . . mascot."

"HAH! Hear that lads?" cried Black Dan, leering round at his crew. "This is their ship's mascot!" He turned back to Captain Rat. "He looks more like a stuffed hot-water bottle to me. Now *this* is what *I* call a ship's mascot. Meet Eric, my parrot."

The parrot took his cigar out of his mouth. "*Tough* Eric," he said. "Not just Eric. *Tough* Eric."

"That's right," said Black Dan. "Tough Eric. Makes your old tortoise look a bit daft, doesn't he? This parrot can bend a penny in his beak."

"That's nothing," said Captain Rat, quick as a flash, "this tortoise used to box for England."

Wedgwood looked startled at this and Black Dan and his crew burst out laughing.

"Him!" cried Black Dan. "He couldn't box his way out of a paper bag! Now this parrot of ours can haul up the anchor all by himself. What d'you think of *that*!"

"I think nothing of that," said Captain Rat (to the amazement of his crew). "This tortoise used to be the strong man in a circus. Before that he was a blacksmith! He was known as the Mighty Wedgwood!"

"What!" hooted Black Dan. "You must be joking! Listen. This parrot is so *tough* that he can crush a walnut in his grasp! Can't you, Tough Eric?"

"Two if I'm in the mood," said Tough Eric, taking a puff on his cigar and blowing the smoke at Captain Rat.

"Well this tortoise is so . . . so . . . *strong* that he can crush *four* walnuts all at once! Whether he's in the mood or not!" cried Captain Rat.

"Two barrels of rum says he can't then!" shouted Black Dan.

"Right! You're on!"

"Right then!"

"Right!"

"Ten minutes warming up time allowed!" announced Black Dan. He and his pirate crew retired to a corner with their parrot while somebody ran out for a bag of walnuts.

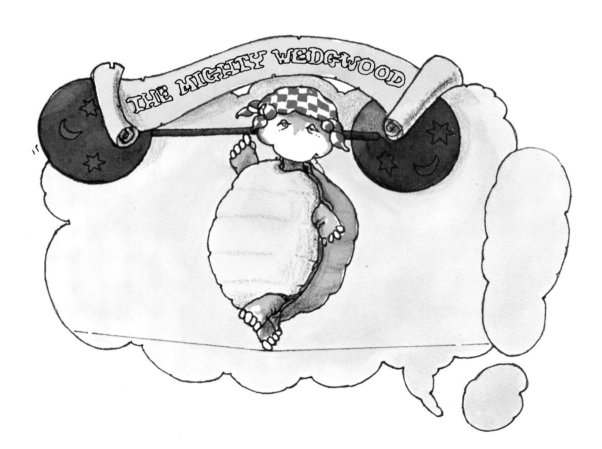

The crew of the Pied Piper looked at their captain in horror.
Then they looked at Wedgwood. Wedgwood looked stunned.
Strong man in a circus? Blacksmith? The *Mighty Wedgwood*?
It was time, he decided, for an early hibernation.

He tucked himself away into his shell to wait for spring.

"Captain Rat," said GBH at last
"have you gone mad? You've just
gambled away our entire ration of
rum for the next six months!"

"Oh dear, oh dear," moaned Captain Rat.
"What have I done? Nobody in their
right mind would take on a bet with
Black Dan! I'm afraid I just got
carried away."

"The only thing that's going to be
carried away as far as *I* can see,"
said Mr Fred Friendly,
"is our rum."

Barnaby Shrew said, "I've got an idea,
I think."

"Don't tell us," said GBH
"It's a long shot,
but it just might work?"
"Exactly," said Barnaby. He picked
up Wedgwood and whispered something
into one of the holes in his shell.
He hoped it was the one that the head
normally poked out of.

The ten minutes were up, the walnuts had arrived and Tough Eric looked in great shape. He did a few wing-springs, beak-ups, and hop-flap-and-squawks along the bar to the cheers of his shipmates.

"SILENCE!" roared Black Dan. "Silence for the Grand Walnut Crushing Contest of the year! In this corner I give you—the one and only, the fabulous, the great—Tough Eric! And in that corner I give you the er . . . *Mighty* Wedgwood. The first prize is two barrels of rum. The second prize is a place at my table tonight. IN THE SOUP! Now then, Tough Eric, do your stuff!"

The parrot put down his cigar and strolled over to the bag of walnuts. Taking out two, he threw one up into the air and caught it in his beak. The other he held in his claws.

Then he squeezed and squeezed until his feathers stood out on end and . . . finally . . .

CRACKKKK! The walnuts exploded like gunshots and a great cheer went up from the pirate crew.

"YAYAYAYAYAY!! Beat that! What a parrot! Two at once! We are the champions!" It sounded like a cricket match.

"Quiet!" shouted Black Dan.
"Now it's the turn of the Mighty Wedgwood.
He will attempt to crush four walnuts.
Four, mind you. No cheating or there'll
be Black Dan to deal with.
And that's no joke, me buckos,
I can tell you!"

Once again there was silence, except for a few sniggers from the pirate crew. Barnaby picked up Wedgwood and put him on the bar. Then he took four walnuts from the bag and put them close together on the floor beneath the bar.

"Now then, Wedgwood," he said.

Wedgwood tucked his head and his legs well into his shell and slowly toppled off the edge of the bar, gathering speed as he fell.

SMASSSHHHHH!! Bits of walnut flew everywhere.

Black Dan and his crew were wild with rage! They roared and cursed and claimed that they had been cheated, but all to no avail. A bet was a bet. Four walnuts had been crushed, two barrels of rum were owing and GBH made sure that they were handed over. You couldn't really argue with GBH.

"BAH!!" cried Black Dan, shaking his fist. "We were tricked! Well, you'll pay for this Captain Rat! I'll . . . I'll . . . WHERE'S THAT PARROT? I'LL MURDER HIM! IT'S THE SOUP BOWL FOR HIM TONIGHT!"

Tough Eric, the parrot, flew straight out of the window when he heard this.

"AFTER HIM!" yelled Black Dan, and he and his crew all scuffled out of the tavern and off down the road.

Captain Rat raised his glass. "My friends," he said, "I think a toast would be in order."

But at this point a bedraggled figure appeared in the doorway. It was Lookout Frank. "I've just seen a one-eyed parrot," he said, "being chased by a bunch of rats all waving soup spoons. Did I miss something?"

"No," said Captain Rat. "In fact you're just in time." He raised his glass once again.

"A toast," he said. "To the Mighty Wedgwood!"
"The Mighty Wedgwood!" came back the reply.
"The *Mighty* Wedgwood?" said Lookout Frank.
"What's *he* been up to?"